W9-CDZ-437

Oranges on Golden Mountain

by Elizabeth Partridge

illustrated by
AKI SOGABE

PUFFIN BOOKS

All of the images in the art, including the black outlines, have been made with paper cut freehand by the illustrator. Watercolor, where used, was applied by airbrush.

PUFFIN BOOKS
Published by the Penguin Group
Penguin Putnam Books for Young Readers,
345 Hudson Street, New York, New York 10014, U.S.A.
Penguin Books Ltd, 80 Strand, London WC2R ORL, England
Penguin Books Australia Ltd, 250 Camberwell Road, Camberwell, Victoria 3124, Australia
Penguin Books Canada Ltd, 10 Alcorn Avenue, Toronto, Ontario, Canada M4V 3B2
Penguin Books (N.Z.) Ltd, 182-190 Wairau Road, Auckland 10, New Zealand

Penguin Books Ltd, Registered Offices: Harmondsworth, Middlesex, England

First published in the United States of America by Dutton Children's Books,
a division of Penguin Putnam Books for Young Readers, 2001
Published by Puffin Books, a division of Penguin Putnam Books for Young Readers, 2003

1 3 5 7 9 10 8 6 4 2

THE LIBRARY OF CONGRESS HAS CATALOGED THE DUTTON EDITION AS FOLLOWS:
Partridge, Elizabeth.
Oranges on Golden Mountain / by Elizabeth Partridge;
illustrated by Aki Sogabe.—1st ed. p. cm.
Summary: When hard times fall on his family, Jo Lee is sent from China to San Francisco,
where he helps his uncle fish and dreams of being reunited with his mother and sister.
ISBN 0-525-46453-0
[1. Emigration and immigration—Fiction. 2. Chinese American—Fiction. 3. San Francisco (Calif.)—Fiction.
4. China—Fiction. 5. Fishing—Fiction. 6. Uncles—Fiction.]
I. Sogabe, Aki, ill. II. Title.
PZ7.P26 Or 2001 [E]—dc21 99-462287

Puffin Books ISBN 0-14-250033-X

Designed by Ellen M. Lucaire

Printed in the United States of America

For my sons,
Will and Felix Ratcliff

E.P.

For my beautiful children,
Steve and Sandy

A.S.

For the second year in a row, no rain fell on Jo Lee's village. The rice ponds dried up and cracked wide open. The sweet-potato vines shriveled and died. Only the orange trees clung to life.

Every day, Jo Lee and his little sister, Mei-Mei, helped in their mother's orchard, carrying buckets of water to each tree. But when the stream dried up, there was no more they could do. The blossoms opened, smelled sweetly of orange, then withered and fell to the ground.

Late one night, Mother knelt on the floor and dug up a small sack full of gold eagle coins. Jo Lee's father had sent the coins from California, a faraway place he called Golden Mountain.

"It's been three years since your father died," his mother told Jo Lee. "All that time I've kept these coins. Now we must use them. I will send you to fish with Fourth Uncle on Golden Mountain." Her mouth trembled, holding her sorrow inside. "At least in the fishing village your belly will always be full."

"I won't go!" Jo Lee cried out. "I don't mind a little hunger!" He threw himself on his mother, wrapping his arms tight around her neck. "I don't even know Fourth Uncle."

"He is your father's brother," she replied. "He will be kind to you." Gently she unwound his arms. "When you are gone, I can give your rice to Mei-Mei."

Jo Lee stood still, the truth of his mother's words sinking inside him like stones falling in water. "I can't go alone," he whispered.

"You are never alone." His mother brushed his cheek with her hand. "Your dream spirit, your Hun, will make sure of that."

天

When it came time for Jo Lee to leave, his mother cut a dozen small branches from her orange trees and bundled them in oilcloth. "Plant them as soon as you can on Golden Mountain," she said. "In five or six years, when they are strong trees, they will be covered with beautiful oranges."

Jo Lee was seasick on the long ship ride to Golden Mountain. He forgot about the orange branches. He forgot about his hunger. He didn't care that he was going to California. He wanted only to be home with his mother and sister.

When Jo Lee's ship arrived in San Francisco, his uncle met him at the customhouse. Everywhere Jo Lee looked, he saw white men with eyes of blue and brown and green. And their hair—red, brown, and even yellow! Some of the men frightened him with their wild, bushy whiskers, harsh voices, and strange smells.

Fourth Uncle brought Jo Lee to the fishing village and gave him the narrow bunk over his own in the sleeping-house. Carefully, Jo Lee unwrapped the oilcloth package and showed his uncle the orange branches.

Fourth Uncle led Jo Lee high up on the hillside above the village where the soil was rich and crumbly and the winds blew gently. Nearby was a spring with clear, sweet water. Together they thrust the branches deep into the ground. Jo Lee wanted to tell Fourth Uncle how the thin brown branches made him long for home. But his uncle was a silent man, and Jo Lee was afraid to speak.

After dinner with the other fishermen, Fourth Uncle took Jo Lee to the letter writer. Jo Lee watched as Fourth Uncle spoke and the letter writer made quick, beautiful brushstrokes with black ink.

"Jo Lee has arrived. He is safe," said Fourth Uncle. "I will teach him to fish from the waters of Golden Mountain. When we have saved enough money, we will send for you and Mei-Mei." Fourth Uncle counted out seven copper coins and handed them to the letter writer.

How long, Jo Lee wondered, until they had enough money?

The next morning, before the rooster's crow split the sky, Fourth Uncle shook Jo Lee awake. They ate big bowls of rice porridge, then slipped onto Fourth Uncle's sampan and sculled out in the marshlands. They heaved the rope nets overboard and waited for the tide to turn.

As the sun edged over the hills, Jo Lee and his uncle pulled up the wet nets, heavy with shrimp and crabs and small fish. The ropes cut into Jo Lee's hands, and his muscles burned with a fiery pain.

It was a good catch. Fourth Uncle nodded in satisfaction. They took it back to the fishing camp, then sculled out again to set their nets.

On the boat the next day, Jo Lee was sore all over, and his hands were rubbed raw. After the nets were heaved overboard, Fourth Uncle motioned him to rest on a pile of rope. Fog settled over the sampan, wrapping them in a wet, gray emptiness.

Jo Lee covered himself with a piece of canvas to keep out the cold fingers of fog. Mother, he thought, if you saw me now. My belly is full, but my heart holds only sorrow.

The boat rose and fell on the swells. In the place between sleep and not-sleep, Jo Lee felt his Hun, the dream spirit, rocking loose of his body. With a little splash, his Hun was over the side of the boat, a tiny flash of silver as he entered the water.

Quick as a mackerel, Jo Lee's dream spirit swam through the gray-green waters of San Francisco Bay, out into the deep blue cold of the Pacific Ocean. Faster and faster he swam, back to China, back to his village. He found his mother and Mei-Mei out in the orange orchard.

"Mother," he murmured, flashing silver in the empty water bucket

she held. "Fourth Uncle and I are working hard, but I am very lonely. When will I see you again?"

His mother's only reply was the *plink-plink* of her tears falling into the empty bucket.

Day after day, Jo Lee helped haul in the nets full of gleaming fish and blue-green shrimp. He carried basketfuls of the shrimp across the splintery pier and threw them into huge pots of boiling water. Then he ladled them out, orange and steaming, to dry under the California sun.

Jo Lee danced on the shrimp in wooden shoes, pressing and stamping, shouting and jumping, until the shrimp snapped out of their shells. Then he sold the shells to the fruit growers, who dug them in around the roots of their apple, pear, peach, and lemon trees. Every coin Jo Lee earned he wrapped in the oilcloth and kept safely under his pillow.

When Jo Lee's work was done, he ran up into the hills to water his orange branches. "Someday," he whispered to the dry brown sticks, "you will be tall, strong trees, full of golden oranges."

By the time of the fall Moon Festival, Jo Lee's back and arms had strengthened, his hands had toughened. Warm winds blew the smell of wild sage from the shore to the sampan. After so long on the boat, Jo Lee was comfortable with Fourth Uncle's silent ways.

When winter storms lashed the fishing village, Jo Lee helped the men drag the boats high up on the shore. Then he sat indoors with the fishermen. He listened to the click and clatter of the mah-jongg tiles, the shouts and cries of the men as they played.

"Join us," said Fourth Uncle, moving over on the bench. "If you are old enough to fish, you are old enough to play mah-jongg."

One night, a fierce storm filled the sky. Lightning danced between the clouds, and thunder shook the thin-walled sleeping-house. Loneliness snatched at Jo Lee as he rolled restlessly from side to side.

Just as he was falling asleep, Jo Lee's Hun pulled loose and shot up into the clouds. His dream spirit jumped on the back of Lung Wong, the Dragon King who brings rain. Together they roared over the storm-tossed Pacific. Inland over China they swept, until the clouds piled up against the high mountains circling Jo Lee's village.

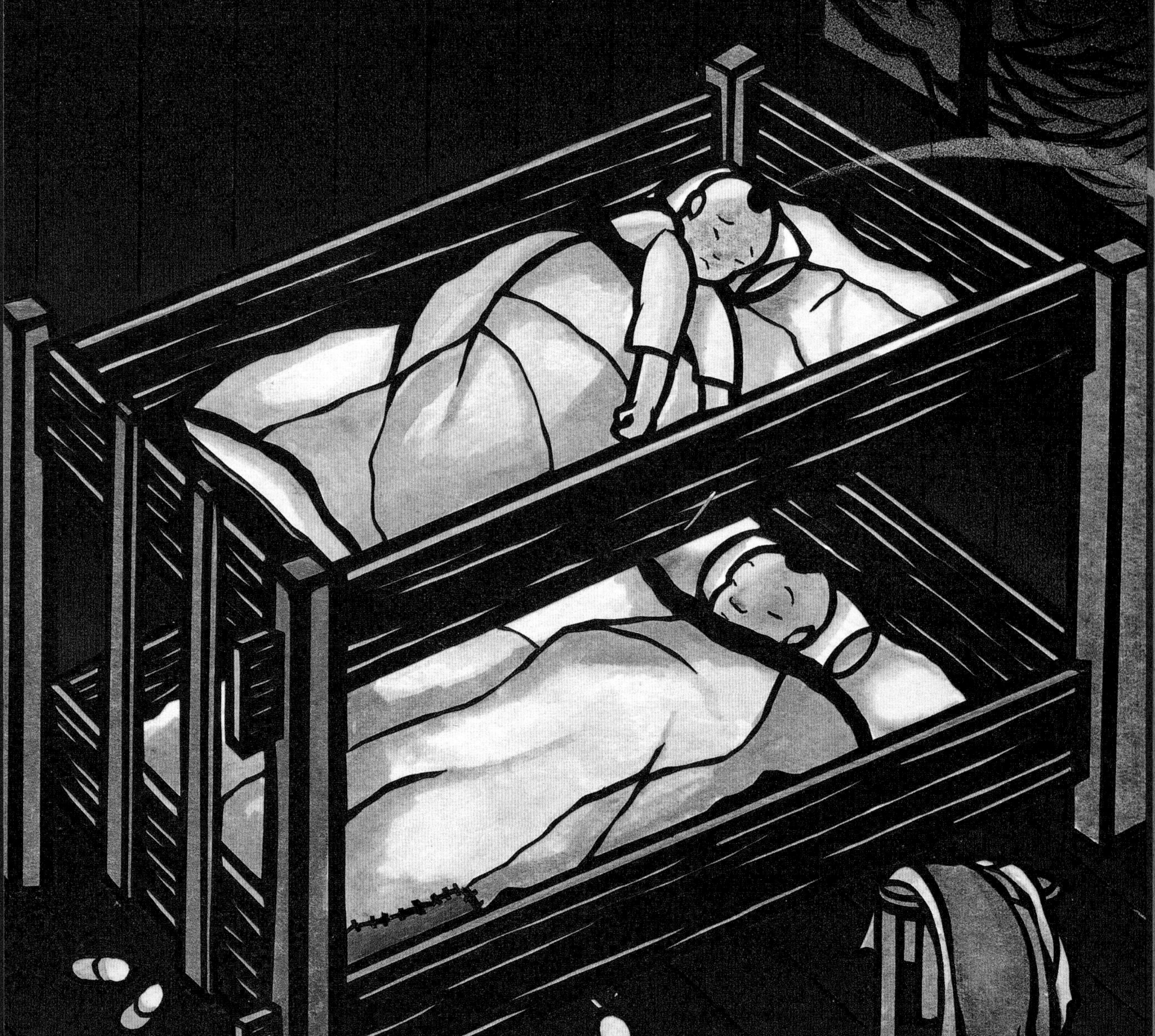

Far below, the villagers rushed back and forth, lighting red strings of firecrackers and beating on metal pots. They called to Lung Wong to bring rain.

"Mother!" Jo Lee shouted, his heart filled with longing. But his mother's ears were full of the wild explosions of the firecrackers, and she never looked up.

When the storms of winter cleared, Jo Lee threw himself into his work. He fished all morning with Fourth Uncle and danced on the shrimp in the afternoon.

The fishermen invited him to go out at night on the big junk. They taught him to build a fire on the bow, throwing on wood to make the flames leap higher and higher. As the fish swam up to the light, Jo Lee pulled in the nets with the other men.

Whenever he could, Jo Lee ran up to the hills. One light, windy day, he discovered small leaves on his orange branches. All spring he watered and tended the new saplings. He pinched off bugs and dug shrimp shells in around the tender young roots.

The saplings flourished, sending out more and more leaves. Finally two tiny blossoms appeared. Jo Lee put his face close and caught the delicate smell, promising of oranges.

He lay on his back under the saplings and watched the clouds drift across the wide blue sky. A breeze blew through the leaves, and birds called in the distance.

As the warmth of the sun soaked into Jo Lee's shirt, his Hun gently rocked loose. On a puff of wind, his dream spirit rose up into the sky and blew back to China.

Dancing and spinning, he swooped down on his mother's small orchard. She stood, empty-handed, the wind blowing through her clothes, rattling the dry leaves in the trees.

"Mother," Jo Lee whispered on the wind. "The orange branches you gave me are strong young saplings now. The first blossoms have come." Soft as a butterfly wing, he brushed her cheek.

His mother's hand flew up to her face.

"Mei-Mei," she called. "Come quickly. The wind brings the smell of orange blossoms and whispers that our fortunes have changed."

That evening, Jo Lee counted out seven copper coins and took them to the letter writer's room.

"Mother," he said, "the fishing is good here. I love the wind and the rain and the sea. Fourth Uncle and I are saving all our money to send for you and Mei-Mei." The letter writer's brush made quick strokes on the paper.

Jo Lee went on. "The soil on Golden Mountain is rich, and the new trees grow well. There will be many oranges when you come to Golden Mountain.

"Your loving son, Jo Lee."

Then Jo Lee ran down to the water and leaped onto the big junk, where the other fishermen were waiting for him.

AFTERWORD

When the California gold rush began in 1849, many Chinese set sail across the Pacific Ocean. These pioneers mostly came from Kwangtung Province. They called California "Gum Shan," or Golden Mountain, because of the gold nuggets buried in the hills and mountains of the state.

For more than three decades, thousands of Chinese men and boys came to Golden Mountain every year. California was Gum Shan in a whole new way—a place that offered tremendous opportunities to make a living, perhaps even become wealthy. The Chinese rushed to the goldfields, worked on the railroads and in factories, ran small businesses, planted California's vast orchards, and fished up and down the Pacific coast. By the late 1880s, there were more than twenty-five Chinese fishing villages like Jo Lee's lining San Francisco Bay. The boys worked long, hard days alongside the adults.

The Chinese usually came as sojourners, intending to return to China after they had made their fortunes. A few of the men brought their wives and children, but most were single. They wore their hair in a long braid, showing obedience to the Chinese emperor. If they died in America, their families had their bones dug up later and sent back to China, so that they could be properly worshiped by their descendants.

Prejudice against the Chinese ran strong. Because they weren't Caucasian, they couldn't become citizens, testify in court, or own land. In 1882, the Chinese Exclusion Act stopped any more Chinese workers from coming to the United States. When Chinese immigration rules relaxed in the twentieth century, the new immigrants to San Francisco were detained on Angel Island for weeks or even months. After careful questioning, some were allowed to enter the country, and some were sent back to China.

According to traditional Chinese philosophy, each person has five spirits. Zhi is willpower; Yi is the capacity to think; Po grants sensations and feelings; and Shen is consciousness. Hun, or the dream spirit, is often translated as "ethereal spirit." The Hun gives the capacity to dream, be courageous, and find a sense of direction in life. During the day, the Hun shines out of a person's eyes. At night, it wanders freely during dreaming.

The early pioneers to California, who came from all parts of the world, needed strong dream spirits to overcome the difficulties of starting new lives far from home.

For more information, old photographs, curriculum ideas, and material on China Camp State Park, see my Web site at www.elizabethpartridge.com

—ELIZABETH PARTRIDGE